The Poor Boy and the Cat

by Damian Harvey and
Becky Davies

W
FRANKLIN WATTS
LONDON•SYDNEY

Once, there was an old man.
He lived in a hut by the sea
with his son, Magnus.

Every night, the old man sat
and counted his money.
He loved counting his money.
But he didn't like spending it.

The old man became very ill.

One night, he said to Magnus,

"When I die, all my money will be yours.

But you must not keep it."

Magnus was sad. He did not like

being poor.

The old man went on, "You must give half of the money to the poor and then throw the rest into the sea. Most of the money will sink, but you can catch and keep anything that swims by."

The old man died.

Magnus gave half of the money

to the poor, just as his father had said.

Then he threw the rest into the sea.

Most of the money sank, but he saw

something white moving in the water.

He bent down and picked it up.

It was a piece of paper with

six silver coins inside.

Magnus looked at the coins.

"This is not much money," he said.

"I do not like being poor.

I will go and seek my fortune."

He walked and walked until he came
to a forest. "I am tired and hungry,"
he said to himself.
Just then, he saw a hut.
He tapped on the door,
and an old woman opened it.
"You must be hungry," said the woman.
"Come in and you can share my dinner."

After dinner, Magnus sat by the fire.

The woman's cat jumped onto his lap.

"I have never had a cat," said Magnus.

"I think he likes me."

"You can have him," said the woman.
"Give me six silver coins."
Magnus gave his six coins to the woman
and he took the cat. Now he had a cat.
But he had no money.

In the morning, Magnus set off again.
He walked and walked until he came
to a hut. "I am tired and hungry,"
he said to himself.
He tapped at the door,
and an old man opened it.
"You must be hungry," said the old man.
"Come in and you can share my dinner."

Magnus told the old man all about
what had happened to him.

"Now, I have no money," said Magnus.

"All I have is a cat."

"Go and see the king," said the old man.

"He may be able to help you."

The next day, Magnus went to see the king.

But the king was not happy.

There were rats everywhere!

There were rats on the floor.

There were rats on the tables.

There were rats eating the king's food
and biting his fingers.

The cat saw the rats.

It hissed and jumped onto the table.

It ran after the rats.

Soon, there was not one rat to be seen.

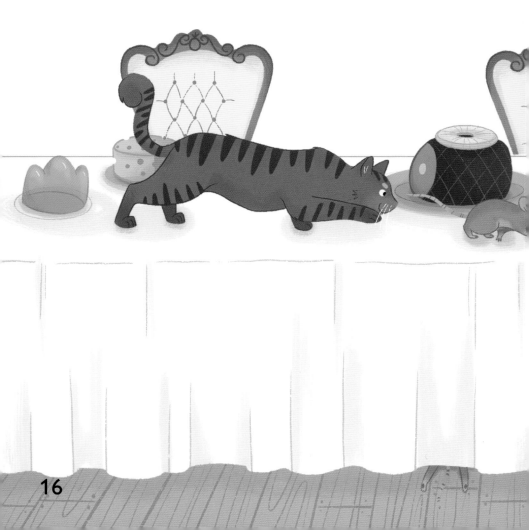

The king was very happy.

"Is this your cat?" he said to Magnus.

"Yes, he is," said Magnus.

"I bought him from an old woman.

I gave her all my money."

"Then you and your cat can stay

in the palace and keep the rats away,"

said the king.

And Magnus and the cat lived
happily ever after in the palace.

Story order

Look at these 5 pictures and captions.
Put the pictures in the right order
to retell the story.

1

Magnus and the cat lived in the palace.

2

Magnus bought a cat from an old woman.

3

The king's palace was full of rats.

4

Magnus found six silver coins.

5

The cat chased the rats away.

Guide for Independent Reading

This series is designed to provide an opportunity for your child to read on their own. These notes are written for you to help your child choose a book and to read it independently.

In school, your child's teacher will often be using reading books which have been banded to support the process of learning to read. Use the book band colour your child is reading in school to help you make a good choice. *The Poor Boy and the Cat* is a good choice for children reading at Turquoise Band in their classroom to read independently. The aim of independent reading is to read this book with ease, so that your child enjoys the story and relates it to their own experiences.

About the book
In this Icelandic tale, a poor boy seeks his fortune with the help of a very useful cat.

Before reading
Help your child to learn how to make good choices by asking: "Why did you choose this book? Why do you think you will enjoy it?" Look at the cover together and ask: "What do you think the story will be about?" Ask your child to think of what they already know about the story context. Then ask your child to read the title aloud.

Ask: "What do you think the cat will be doing in the story?"

Remind your child that they can sound out a word in syllable chunks if they get stuck.

Decide together whether your child will read the story independently or read it aloud to you.

During reading

Remind your child of what they know and what they can do independently. If reading aloud, support your child if they hesitate or ask for help by telling them the word. If reading to themselves, remind your child that they can come and ask for your help if stuck.

After reading

Support comprehension by asking your child to tell you about the story. Use the story order puzzle to encourage your child to retell the story in the right sequence, in their own words. The correct sequence can be found on the next page.

Help your child think about the messages in the book that go beyond the story and ask: "Do you think Magnus would have found his fortune without the cat's help?"

Give your child a chance to respond to the story: "Did you have a favourite part? What did you think would happen when Magnus went to the palace?"

Extending learning

Help your child understand the story structure by using the same sentence patterning and adding different elements. "Let's make up a new story about Magnus and the cat. Where will they go? Who could they help?"

In the classroom, your child's teacher may be teaching about recognising punctuation marks. Ask your child to identify speech marks in the story and look at how they are used to show when a character is speaking.

Franklin Watts
First published in Great Britain in 2022
by Hodder & Stoughton

Copyright © Hodder & Stoughton Limited, 2022

Series Editors: Jackie Hamley and Melanie Palmer
Series Advisors and Development Editors: Dr Sue Bodman and Glen Franklin
Series Designers: Cathryn Gilbert and Peter Scoulding

A CIP catalogue record for this book is
available from the British Library.

ISBN 978 1 4451 8423 4 (hbk)
ISBN 978 1 4451 8424 1 (pbk)
ISBN 978 1 4451 8505 7 (library ebook)
ISBN 978 1 4451 8504 0 (ebook)

Printed in China

Franklin Watts
An imprint of
Hachette Children's Group
Part of Hodder & Stoughton
Carmelite House
50 Victoria Embankment
London EC4Y 0DZ

An Hachette UK Company
www.hachette.co.uk

www.reading-champion.co.uk

Answer to Story order: 4, 2, 3, 5, 1